Haywire

Adapted by Beth Beechwood

Based on the series created by Todd J. Greenwald

Part One is based on the episode, "I Almost Drowned in a Chocolate Fountain,"
Written by Gigi McCreery & Perry Rein

Part Two is based on the episode, "Curb Your Dragon," Written by Gigi McCreery & Perry Rein

New York

Copyright © 2008 Disney Enterprises, Inc.

All rights reserved. Published by Disney Press, an imprint of Disney Book Group.
No part of this book may be reproduced or transmitted in any form or by any
means, electronic or mechanical, including photocopying, recording,
or by any information storage and retrieval system, without
written permission from the publisher. For information address
Disney Press, 114 Fifth Avenue, New York, New York 10011-5690.

Printed in the United States of America

First Edition
1 3 5 7 9 10 8 6 4 2

Library of Congress Catalog Card Number: 2007942960
ISBN: 978-1-4231-1290-7

For more Disney Press fun, visit www.disneybooks.com
Visit DisneyChannel.com

PART
ONE

Chapter One

Alex Russo hurried down the stairs of Tribeca Prep. She had just spotted her best friend, Harper Evans, and couldn't wait to tell her the news. She approached Harper, waving a piece of paper in the air. "Check it out!" she shouted happily. "I got an F on my Spanish midterm!"

Harper was puzzled. "Why are you so happy about it?" she asked.

Alex smiled. "Because Riley got an F, too. That means he's been paying as much attention to me as I've been to him." She let out a big sigh, as an image of her crush flashed through her mind. "Failing Spanish is hard work," she said dramatically.

Again, Harper was confused by her friend's reaction. "How is failing Spanish hard work?"

Alex gave Harper a serious look and tried to explain. Sometimes her best friend had trouble catching on to what Alex was trying to tell her.

"Every day I show up late so he'll definitely notice me. Then, I 'forget' my textbook, so we have to share one. And finally, I let the teacher catch us passing notes, so she keeps us both after class," Alex said.

Harper nodded sympathetically. "That *is* hard work. You must be exhausted," she said.

Just then, Riley walked up to them.

"Hey, Alex," Riley said casually. "A bunch of us are going to this cool restaurant, Medium Rare, on Friday night," he said. "Wanna come?"

Alex pretended to know the restaurant well, even though she had never heard of it before in her life. After all, she *did* live in New York City, and she didn't want Riley to think she wasn't hip to the coolest places to hang out. "Oh, sure," she said with a smile. "Medium Rare. I go there all the time."

"But it's new," Riley pointed out. "Friday's opening night."

Uh-oh, Alex thought. She quickly corrected herself. "Oh, Medium *Rare*," she said with a laugh. "I thought you said Medium *Roar*. You know, like, bigger than a kitten, and smaller than a lion, you know—like a cougar. Anyway, it's out by the zoo." She gave Riley a confident smile.

He smiled back and then turned to Harper. "You can come, too," he said politely.

"Well, I might as well," Harper shrugged, "since my best friend never took me to Medium Roar," she said with a huff. Harper

5

once again missed the whole thing and bought Alex's convoluted story.

After agreeing to meet the girls at Medium Rare on Friday night, Riley walked off, leaving them to discuss what had just occurred.

"Look at that," Alex commented. "All those hours I didn't spend on studying totally paid off."

But Harper was barely paying attention. She was distracted by the boy walking toward them. "Oh, no! Here comes your brother," she said to Alex. "I think he's coming over here. Oh, he's so cute. I never know what to say to him."

Though Alex could not, for the life of her, understand the crush Harper had on her older brother, Justin, she tried to help. "Uh, just talk about current events. He *loves* current events," she suggested.

"Hey, guys," Justin said cheerfully.

"Alex failed her Spanish midterm!" Harper blurted out.

Justin looked over at Alex in amusement.

Alex turned to glare at her friend. "Not *that* current!"

Oh, great, Alex thought to herself. If Justin tells Mom and Dad about this, I'm definitely not going to Medium Rare on Friday night. Or *anywhere* for that matter! Even though Alex, her brother Justin, and her younger brother Max had wizard powers that they inherited from their dad, there were still some things that Alex couldn't pull off. Sure, sometimes she could log onto her wizard computer and make a store appear right in front of her, or clone herself so she could be in two places at once. But convincing her parents that failing Spanish is not a big deal? *So* not possible.

I hope Justin keeps his big mouth shut, Alex thought. If not, I'm going to have to come up with a plan, and fast!

Chapter Two

Later that day after school, Alex and Justin came home to find their brother, Max, hanging out in the living room of their apartment with their parents. Mr. and Mrs. Russo had just come upstairs from the Waverly Sub Station, the sandwich shop that they owned and ran. It was a bright, fun place decorated to look like an old subway car. The Russo siblings helped out their parents at the restaurant some days after school and on weekends.

"Hey," Alex piped up. "Guess who got asked out on a date today? Me or Justin?"

"Not Justin," Max quipped.

Alex's mom gave her a stern look. "I'm more interested in learning about what happened in Spanish class," Theresa Russo said.

"Uh, yeah," her dad Jerry said slowly. "We heard you failed."

Alex didn't have to be a genius to see her parents were really upset with her. "That's right," she admitted. "I did fail. But I can explain." She took a deep breath. "There I was . . . studying as hard as I ever have. But I couldn't concentrate, because right outside that window, Justin and Max were playing paintball, and I didn't want to ruin their fun." If she could get her dad to focus on her brothers playing paintball where they weren't supposed to, maybe he would forget all about her failing grade.

"Paintball on the terrace?" Mr. Russo

asked loudly. "I told you not to, because it chips the bricks!" He walked over to the curtains that were drawn over the sliding-glass doors leading to the terrace and shook his head in disbelief.

"No, no! We didn't play paintball!" Max exclaimed, trying desperately to defend himself and his brother.

Mr. Russo pulled back the curtains, revealing paintball blobs splattered all over the glass doors. He turned to the boys and gave them his angriest scowl. "You guys are gonna scrub that terrace until those bricks sparkle."

"Shiny bricks coming up," Max said enthusiastically as he hurried off to get cleaning supplies. The punishment could have been worse. . . .

Meanwhile, Mrs. Russo had not been distracted from Alex's grades. "I'm so sorry. Your failing Spanish is all my fault," she said sadly.

Alex was not sure what her mom meant, but she thought she'd better jump on it anyway. "Oh, okay. You're right. It *is* your fault." Alex couldn't believe how well this was going!

"It is?" Mr. Russo asked.

"Of course it is," Mrs. Russo told her husband. She looked over at Alex. "I'm going to call your Spanish teacher and tell her what a horrible role model I've been," she said. She headed over to the phone and dialed. As she waited for Alex's teacher to answer, she explained. "Here I am, a proud Latina, and I haven't been sharing your Mexican heritage with you. I should be speaking Spanish around the house, and we should be making our own homemade tortillas!" she cried dramatically. She paused for a minute to think about what she had just said. "Oh, my gosh, that's a lot of work," she mumbled. "Let's just start with the Spanish. Okay?" She laughed.

Just then, Alex's Spanish teacher answered

the phone. "Mrs. Chow," Mrs. Russo said pleasantly.

While Mrs. Russo spoke with Alex's teacher, Justin approached his sister. "Hey, thanks a lot. You busted us for paintball." He gave her a mean look.

"Justin—" Alex protested.

But Justin didn't wait for Alex to make up an excuse. He stormed out of the room.

Meanwhile, Mrs. Russo was ending her phone conversation with Mrs. Chow. "Yes, it is embarrassing. . . . Thank you. I . . . I mean, *gracias*," she said with a laugh. She hung up the phone and turned to Alex. "Good news! Mrs. Chow said she'd give you a retest!" she exclaimed excitedly.

Before Alex could respond, her dad chimed in. "Great! You're not going anywhere with your friends until you get your grades up."

"Jerry, this is my responsibility," Mrs. Russo interrupted. She turned her attention back to Alex. "Don't worry, honey. I'm gonna help you with your *español*."

"Okay, that's fine, but I really need help with my Spanish, too," Alex said. She really didn't know any words in Spanish at *all*.

"*Español* is Spanish," Mrs. Russo explained.

"*Español* is Spanish for what?" Alex asked innocently.

Mrs. Russo sighed. "This is going to be hard."

"No, it's not. It will be easy," Alex said. "We're going to whip through this, and I'm going to go on my date with Riley on Friday."

Mr. Russo was skeptical. "I got some Spanish for you: No way, José," he said with a chuckle.

Later that day, the Russo kids' gathered in the lair for their wizard lessons. They had lessons every Tuesday and Thursday afternoon after school in their basement. They called it a lair because it was filled with cool gadgets, books of spells, and other magical things. When they were in the lair, anything was possible!

But today, they were sitting around, waiting for their father's lecture to conclude. Sometimes, magic was just like any other school subject—boring.

"And finally, did you guys know that in the magic world there's a place where you can get information on any subject quickly and easily?" Mr. Russo asked.

"You mean like the Internet?" Justin suggested.

Max took this opportunity to voice a request that was becoming all-too familiar. "Speaking of the Internet, when am I getting a computer in my room?"

Mr. Russo turned to Justin and sighed. "It's cooler than the Internet," and then turning to Max, he added, "Never." Max grumbled, but was quickly distracted by his dad's excitement.

"Come on, guys!" Mr. Russo exclaimed,

waving the kids over to a portal wall. "Check it out!" he exclaimed. "You just pull this lever, and it generates Pocket Elves that have in-depth knowledge on any subject you could ever need to know about. Whatever Pocket Elf you want, it comes shooting out of the magic portal."

Mr. Russo grabbed a catcher's mask and mitt near him, and pulled the lever. Suddenly, out flew a flying egg-shaped container! Mr. Russo expertly caught it in his mitt.

"Whoa!" Max exclaimed, his eyes wide with amazement.

Mr. Russo proudly turned around, holding the container in hand. "The best way to teach you about Pocket Elves is from a Pocket Elf himself."

Still recovering from the sudden appearance of what looked like an average container, the kids headed over to the coffee table. Mr. Russo put the little container down and unscrewed the top. Just then, a tiny man popped out. He stood about six inches tall. "Oh, he's so cool!" Alex gasped.

Justin and Max agreed, oohing and aahing at the sight of the elf.

"Good day," he announced. " I am the Pocket Elf who specializes in history and use of Pocket Elves. Now, Pocket Elves are useful for research on everything from magical illnesses to magical creatures. Any questions?"

Alex raised her hand. "Yes, little lady in the attractive hat," he said, complimenting her on her attire. Alex was wearing a bright orange knit newsboy cap.

"Are there Pocket Elves for subjects non-magical?" she asked.

"Uh, because of the Magic World Equal Opportunity Act, there are Pocket Elves on all subjects. Shaquille O'Neal? I know his Pocket Elf." He laughed. "He owes me an auto-graphed shoe that I'm going to be living in."

Justin raised his hand next. "Yes, boy with the eighties hair," the elf said, calling on Justin.

Justin decided to ignore the elf's comment. "Uh, how many Pocket Elves can you check out at once?"

Mr. Russo interrupted. "None," he said. "They're not library books." Just then Max started to unwrap a piece of chocolate. The elf spotted it immediately.

"Can I have some of that?" he asked Max casually.

"Sure," Max said and started to offer a piece to the elf.

Just then, Mr. Russo jumped up and made a dramatic interception of the chocolate. "No! Wait!" He turned to the elf. "What are you doing?" he shrieked.

The Pocket Elf shrugged. He turned to the kids. "Oh, did I mention that Pocket Elves are not supposed to have chocolate?" he asked innocently.

Justin looked over at the elf curiously. "What happens if he has chocolate?" he asked, turning to his father.

"To you and me, chocolate is a delicious treat often used to say 'I'm sorry' to a loved one," Mr. Russo explained. "But to this little guy, it's like lighting a fuse on a crazy bomb."

This was too exciting for Max. "Then let's set this baby off and give him some chocolate!" he said with glee.

The Pocket Elf smiled. If he played his cards right, maybe he could get his hands on that chocolate after all. "You know, in this controlled environment, it might be helpful to the students if someone were to give me some chocolate," he said innocently. "Purely for educational purposes," he added.

"Yeah, come on," Max urged his dad.

"Come on, Dad," Alex pleaded.

"All right," Mr. Russo said finally, though he was still a bit worried as to what would happen. "For educational purposes, we'll do this." He turned to Alex and said, "Honey, grab me that box." He looked around the room. "Uh, legs up off the floor," he instructed, "button your collars all the way up; no open-toed shoes, right? And whatever you do," he said with a worried chuckle, "do *not* let a Pocket Elf bite you."

The Pocket Elf smiled. "Before we get started, I just wanna say thank you so much for the chocolate. He started to laugh maniacally as Mr. Russo lifted him up and dropped him in the box. After a few moments, the box began to shake so violently that Mr. Russo could hardly hold it shut! Alex, Justin, and Max couldn't believe their eyes.

"Dad!" Alex shouted.

"Proceed to the exit in an orderly fashion!" Mr. Russo cried frantically. "Go! Go!" he yelled, as the kids ran out of the lair and back into the safety of their living room. Their dad came running in a little while later, completely out of breath. He had successfully managed to contain the Pocket Elf in the box back in the lair. Apparently, the experiment wasn't such a great idea after all!

Chapter Three

That evening, Mrs. Russo sat on the sofa, quizzing Alex. She was determined for her daughter to get a good grade on her Spanish retest.

"Okay, let's review," she said. She pointed to the lamp. *"Como se dice?"*

Alex looked over at the lamp. *"Lamp-ito!"* she exclaimed.

"Lampara," Mrs. Russo corrected her and walked over to the kitchen counter. "It's okay.

Uh . . . *como se dice*?" she asked, holding up a coffee cup.

Alex didn't do much better this time. "*Cup-ito*?" she offered.

Mrs. Russo sighed. "Oh, boy," she said, shaking her head.

Alex was completely frustrated. "My test is tomorrow, and if I don't pass, I won't be able to go on my date with Riley on Friday," she whined.

"I know, honey. Maybe we can bake cookies on Friday," Mrs. Russo said with a sympathetic smile.

Alex couldn't believe her bad luck. She was determined to go out with Riley. How was she going to pull this off?

The next day Alex was about to open her locker when Harper walked up to her. She was wearing a bright yellow T-shirt decorated with giant pink watermelons. Harper had a very unique sense of style.

"What are you thinking about wearing on Friday?" Harper asked. But before her friend could answer, Harper went on. "I think I'm gonna stick with this whole fruit theme, you know? I don't want us to be wearing the same thing."

Alex just smiled. She didn't have the heart to tell Harper that sometimes her fashion choices were a bit, um, *quirky*.

"Oh. Okay, well, you can wear it this time," Alex said, referring to Harper's brightly colored shirt. "And the time after that," she added jokingly.

Harper grinned. "We're set. And you've got your Spanish retest covered, right?" she asked.

"I'm taking it during study hall," Alex told her. "Consider this test *pass-itoed*."

"*Pass-itoed?*" Harper asked quizzically. Even *she* knew that wasn't a word. "Okay. See you later," she said, walking away.

Alex turned and opened her locker. Sitting

atop her pile of books was a Pocket Elf. She had snuck into the lair before school and hid him in her backpack. He was wearing a large sombrero and a white suit. Luckily, no one had seen a thing!

"Ah, *senorita,* you are so lucky to have me as your Spanish Language Pocket Elf," he said in a thick accent.

Alex quickly looked around to see if anyone had spotted the elf. That would be disastrous on so many levels! First, if she got caught cheating on her test, she would be in *big* trouble. But secondly, and most importantly, was the fact that her magical abilities were to be kept a secret at all costs. If anyone found out—well, it would change everything!

"Keep quiet, elf," Alex demanded. Then she picked him up and tossed him in her backpack. "Just stay in here and zip it!"

From inside her bag she heard the elf reading aloud. "Ooh. A journal. 'Dear diary,

Riley is such a hottie with his new haircut. . . .'"

Alex couldn't believe it. The elf was reading her personal thoughts about Riley! She purposely bumped into a garbage can with her backpack as she passed it.

"Ow!" the elf cried.

"Oops," Alex said with a grin.

Taking a deep breath, Alex headed into study hall to take her test. She walked out forty-five minutes later, with a smug grin on her face. The Pocket Elf had given her all the answers that she needed to at least get her a passing grade. Now, the only thing standing between her and her Friday-night date was an elf she needed to get rid of before anyone found out about it.

As soon as she got home, she headed straight for the lair and dumped the elf, who had fallen asleep, onto the coffee table. She let out a big sigh of relief. "Okay, wake up, *senor-ito*. We're home!" she announced.

"Can I make you breakfast, *chiquita*?" the elf said. "*Huevos rancheros*? Perhaps you can dine on that while I enjoy some semisweet chocolate that you give me." He gave her a sly smile.

"Okay, your Spanish confuses me, and I'm not giving you chocolate." Alex had learned her lesson. Pocket Elves and chocolate were a messy—and—scary combination.

"Good. It was a test," the elf said. "And you passed. That's why I want to grow old with you, *chiquita*."

Alex rolled her eyes. This elf was too much! It was time for him to go back in the portal, before she got caught.

But just then, Justin came into the room. He thought he had heard his dad's voice.

"Dad, we finished cleaning the bricks—" He stopped in midsentence when he spotted Alex, who was trying to hide the elf behind her back.

"Is that a Pocket Elf?" Justin asked accusingly.

The elf muttered something in Spanish and Justin's eyes grew wide. So *that* was what Alex was doing with a Pocket Elf. He almost clapped his hands in excitement. His sister was *so* busted! "Cheater!" Justin shouted out.

"I didn't cheat. I just . . ." Alex tried to counter her brother's accusations, but Justin just interrupted her.

"Cheater!" he yelled again.

"I just used the Pocket Elf to get the answers right on the test," Alex admitted. "So what?"

" 'So what' is you're in trouble," Justin scoffed.

"Come on, Justin. Please don't tell Dad," Alex pleaded.

"Give me one good reason why I shouldn't," her brother replied. "You ratted me out for paintball, and I've spent the last two days cleaning bricks."

For once, Alex was speechless. She couldn't think of any way to convince Justin that he shouldn't tell on her.

Suddenly, Justin thought of a different idea. "You know what? I'm not gonna tell on you," he said.

"Thanks," Alex responded, visibly relieved.

"I'm gonna get even!" he announced.

This time Alex scoffed. "Okay, that'll never happen. Remember the last time you got even with me? I got the bigger bedroom. And you got what?" she prodded.

"To ride shotgun on that one trip to the outlet mall," Justin recalled with embarrassment.

"Exactly," Alex said smugly. "Some things never change." She walked out of the lair and back upstairs toward her room. She had more important things to deal with—like picking out an outfit for Friday night. She wasn't the least bit worried about Justin and his attempt to get even. Nobody was going to stand in her way of her fun Friday night.

Chapter Four

The next day, after school, Alex couldn't wait to get to the Waverly Sub Station. As Alex walked in, she proudly waved her test paper in the air. "Guess who got an A on her makeup test?" Alex beamed.

"Really?" her mother asked in disbelief. "Oh, let me see that," she said, grabbing the test from Alex. He mother gasped as she looked it over. "Wow!"

"Oh, you know what the Spanish say," Alex quipped, before realizing she had absolutely no idea what the Spanish say. Luckily at that moment, her dad walked in.

"Hey, Dad!" Alex called out. "Guess what? I got an A on my makeup test, and I'm going to go on my date with Riley!"

Mr. Russo groaned. "Wasn't expecting this," he muttered. "Very disappointed."

Alex was thoroughly confused. "That I passed?" she asked.

"Yeah," her father confessed. "Because now we have to have," he paused for dramatic effect, "the date talk." He pulled up a chair, and they sat down at one of the tables. "All right, here goes. . . . A lot of times, when you're out alone with a boy—" Mr. Russo was about to continue when Alex interrupted him.

"Alone? What are you talking about? We're not going to be alone," she said.

"You're not?" he asked in surprise.

"No. Harper, Stacy, Jeff, Cassandra, Terry, Samantha, Chris, Noah, and Kelly will be there, too," she replied.

Mr. Russo couldn't help but laugh. "And you call *that* a date?" he asked, unable to contain his laughter. "That's not what I called a date when I was a kid."

"What was a date when you were a kid?" Alex asked him.

Mr. Russo stammered a bit. This wasn't a question he wanted to answer. "You know what? You're right. That *is* a date."

Friday night finally arrived. Coming downstairs, Justin joined Max on the living room sofa. "Is she still getting ready for her date?" his younger brother asked.

"Yeah," Justin answered. "And she's gonna be a while, too. I tied all her belts in one big knot." He smiled mischieviously. That wasn't even the worst of it.

The brothers had a far grander scheme to sabotoge Alex's night. "Now, this is getting even. When that Pocket Elf goes wild on her date, she'll wish she was home making us cookies," Max said impishly.

Justin suddenly heard his sister's footsteps. "Oh, shh . . . shh, here she comes," he said to Max.

Alex entered the room carrying a giant tangle of belts. She waved it at her brothers. "Oh, Justin got even with me," she said sarcastically. "Tied all my belts together so I'd be fashionably late for my date. Wow, you got me. You're *so* clever."

"Wow, I don't even know why I try," Justin said, playing along. "Well, at least you can relax. There's nothing else to worry about," he assured her. He couldn't wait for her to find out what getting even *really* meant!

"Yep," Max agreed, "nothing's gonna go

wrong on your date as long as you take your purse and—" He was cut off when Justin elbowed him in the side.

Alex rolled her eyes. Sometimes she had no idea what Max was even talking about. Brothers, she thought, can be so immature. But she didn't have the time or the inclination to try and figure it out. Grabbing her purse, she headed toward the door. "All right, Dad," she called when Mr. Russo walked in the room. "I'm leaving."

"Okay, honey," he said, giving her a kiss. "Have fun on your date."

Alex happily headed out to meet up with Riley and her friends. She couldn't wait to get the night started!

Alex and Harper stood at the hostess stand of Medium Rare with their entire group behind them.

"Welcome to Medium Rare. How many?"

she asked with a bored tone in her voice.

"Ten," Alex said, but then thought for a moment. "But Lauren and Meg might come, and if they do, Kelly will definitely leave."

Harper chimed in. "And if Kelly leaves, Stacy will call Francis, who will definitely show up, which means I have to leave, 'cause we're fighting. How many is that?" she asked, looking at Alex.

"It's either ten, eleven, thirteen, or twelve," Alex said with a smile.

The hostess grimaced and walked the group over to their table.

Once they were all seated, Alex leaned in toward Riley. "So, I heard you got your learner's permit!" she said excitedly.

"Oh, yeah. Check it out!" Riley exclaimed, proudly pulling out his permit to show her.

"Oh, that's a *great* picture of you," Alex replied. "But you know what would make it better? Me in it *with* you." She smiled.

"Uh, I don't think they do that," Riley said with a laugh.

Harper looked over at Riley and Alex. They seemed to be having such a good time. She leaned closer to Alex. "You and Riley are *so* clicking," she said with a grin.

"He's totally cool," Alex swooned. "And he can drive with a parent or guardian during any daylight hour!" Alex couldn't believe how well the night was going. And all because of the Pocket Elf, she thought slyly.

Back at home, Justin and Max sat on the sofa practically shaking in anticipation. They couldn't wait for Alex to get home so they could hear all the details of their perfectly planned disaster.

"She's gonna be so embarrassed," Max said gleefully. "We're geniuses."

"How much chocolate did you put in her purse?" Justin asked.

Max pulled a candy bar out of his pocket and held it up. "About this much." He paused for a minute, realizing he had made a very big mistake. "Oops. I was supposed to put *this* chocolate in her purse, wasn't I?"

"That was your *only* part of the plan, genius!" Justin exclaimed.

"I told you not to trust me with a complicated plan like this," Max argued.

"What's so complicated about putting that chocolate in her purse?" Justin asked.

Max tried to come up with an explanation. "That I had to *remember* to put this chocolate in her purse," he finally replied.

Justin groaned. He had to think of a way to fix this mess *immediately*! This was the perfect opportunity to get even with Alex and he wasn't going to waste it. "We gotta get to that restaurant and get that chocolate in her purse," he said to Max. Moments later, they were out the door.

Chapter Five

Meanwhile at Medium Rare, Alex had no inkling of what her brothers' were planning because she hadn't opened up her purse yet. If she had, she would have discovered the Pocket Elf they had planted there. But she was so busy fawning over Riley she couldn't think about anything else.

"I was thinking, when I get my car, I'm going to get a little license plate key chain with your name on it. Is that cool?" Riley asked Alex.

Alex tried to be nonchalant, but she couldn't believe what she had just heard! "I guess," she said casually. "If you want." She turned to Harper and gasped with excitement. "Harper, did you hear that? He's gonna put my name on his key chain!"

"I'm gonna cry. I promised I wouldn't cry," Harper said, getting all choked up.

At that moment, Justin and Max entered the restaurant and immediately spotted their sister. "There she is! Duck!" Justin directed. The two brothers hid behind a dessert cart.

"Excuse me, what are you doing?" a waiter asked them.

"Trying to figure out how to get chocolate into *that* purse," Justin said, pointing in Alex's directon.

"Why?" the waiter asked.

"To mess with our sister," Max said matter-of-factly.

The waiter grinned. "I have a sister," he said. "Get in."

The guys hopped under the curtain of the cart, and the waiter pushed them over to Alex's table. Max quickly dropped the candy bar in Alex's purse without her noticing. But suddenly, the chocolate bar popped right back out. Or rather, someone *threw* it out.

Max threw it back in. But again, it flew right back out! He and Justin looked at each other in confusion. Pocket Elves loved chocolate! What was going on?

Very carefully, Justin pulled Alex's purse inside the cart. Looking inside, they saw the elf angrily waving them off. "No *mas*! No *mas*! As much as I want, I cannot," he pleaded quietly.

"Oh, great," Justin grumbled. "We picked the one elf that's on a diet."

"Oh, come on, elf, eat it! You know you want to," Max coaxed.

The elf continued to shake his head no but

slowly his shaking grew less determined. The chocolate smelled so good. The elf couldn't resist any longer. Reaching out, he grabbed the chocolate and chomped down. "Oh, this is good," he said, chewing loudly. "Oh, this is really good. You guys probably want to get away from me right now," he warned.

Justin didn't want to stick around to see what was going to happen next, at least not up close and personal. "Home, Jeeves," he directed the waiter. The waiter pushed them back in the direction of the hostess station, where they could watch from a safe distance.

Back at the table, unaware of the sabotage, Alex and Riley were still busy chatting and laughing. Harper looked at her friend happily. Suddenly realizing her lips felt chapped, she went to grab some lip balm from her purse and she realized she had left it at home. "Alex, do you have any lip gloss?" she asked.

"Let me look," Alex said, reaching into her

purse. "Ow!" she cried. "Something bit me!" She looked inside and spotted the culprit. It was the same elf who had helped her cheat on her Spanish test. "What are you doing here? And why did you bite me?" she hissed.

"I'm eating chocolate like there's no tomorrow!" the elf replied, practically bursting with excitement. "And you can't have any, you can't have any," he said in a singsong voice, growing more and more frantic with each bite.

"I don't want any of your chocolate," Alex whispered nervously. She had no idea what to do about this crazy elf in her purse! If Riley and the other kids spotted him, she'd be in big trouble.

Back underneath the cart, Max was not happy about what he was seeing—or rather— *not* seeing. The elf was supposed to cause a scene! "It didn't go crazy," he whispered to Justin, "it just bit her." It looked like their plan was a bust. Sighing, they turned back to the table and waited. . . . hopefully.

Back at the table, Riley had moved on from keychains and was now bragging about the new car he would get once he got his license.

"I wanna get my ride in midnight blue," he said to Alex.

"That would look great with my eyes," Alex said absently. Her eyes were glued to the chocolate dessert the waiter had just placed in front of Riley. "Can I have a bite of that?"

"Sure," Riley said, motioning to his plate.

Alex smacked her lips. She was so focused on eating she was barely paying attention to Riley at all. "What color interior?" she asked as she started to shovel ice cream into her mouth. Suddenly, she was ravenously hungry for chocolate.

"I'm thinking tan leather," he said, looking at her strangely.

"I'm more of a dark leather person," Alex

said, finishing the last bite of Riley's dessert. She then turned her attention to Harper's dessert. "Can I have that?"

"Okay, sure," Harper slowly replied. She didn't really know what was going on, either. Her best friend was acting like she hadn't eaten in weeks!

Meanwhile, Alex rambled on and on about colors. "Mmm. Ooh! You know what's not a good color combo? Our school colors," she said, smacking her lips. "Blue and gold. Ick. That's why I'm not a cheerleader. I should start a school petition to change our colors to midnight blue and chocolate," she said.

She had now moved on to someone else's dessert. It was a chocolate milk shake with a chocolate straw. Alex went to take a sip and realized the straw was edible. She took a bite. Then she took a huge bite of the shake's chocolate cup, too. Soon her face was completely covered in chocolate!

"That's an interesting story," Riley said apprehensively. He liked a girl with an appetite, but this was a little out of control!

"Hold that thought," Alex said. She grabbed another dessert and took a huge bite. "You were saying?" she asked, chocolate dripping down her face.

Riley laughed nervously. He couldn't believe what he was seeing. He tried to ignore Alex's strange behavior and continue their conversation.

"I wanna get the tires for my ride bigger in the back and smaller in the front. It's called 'chopper style,'" he said, hoping that Alex would suddenly return to normal.

But Alex continued to make no sense at all. "Oh. I hope it doesn't run on chocolate," Alex commented. "That would be a waste of chocolate." Suddenly, she spotted a couple at the table next to theirs who were eating cake. Alex got up and headed over to them.

"Oh! Happy anniversary!" Alex exclaimed cheerfully. "I knew you two would work out. Can I have some?" she asked. She looked eagerly at their dessert and didn't wait for their permission to dig in. She picked up the rest of the cake and shoved the huge chunk in her mouth! She was completely out of control!

Just when everyone thought she had exhausted all the surrounding dessert possibilities, Alex spotted another one that she couldn't resist. "Oh, wait, I want that!" she exclaimed, running over to a waiter who was carrying a giant bowl of liquid chocolate. She snatched it out of his hands.

Riley turned to Harper. "Is she okay?" he asked. His eyes were filled with a mixture of disgust and disbelief.

Harper didn't know how to respond. She thought fast. "You know us girls." She shrugged. "Gotta have our chocolate."

Unaware of the major scene she was

causing, Alex looked at the large bowl of chocolate and smiled. "Now we're talkin'," she said, before taking a huge gulp. Liquid chocolate began to spill everywhere! As she continued to drink from the bowl, a waiter suddenly hurried by and bumped into her. She lost her grip, and the bowl crashed to the floor.

"Does anyone know the chocolate slide?" Alex called out. She dove into the chocolate that covered the floor and slid around in it happily.

From their hiding spot in the cart, Justin and Max watched the chaos ensue. This was better than anything they imagined. It was a total disaster!

"Revenge is sweet!" Max exclaimed.

"And sticky," Justin added.

Just then, Alex stood up. "That was fun," she said, looking around.

But Riley didn't agree. This was the absolute worst date. Talk about messy! He wanted to get out of there—fast! Standing up, he threw down some money and headed toward the nearest exit.

Harper knew Alex must be feeling weird to act that way. "She had a really nice time." Harper called to Riley. "And she totally wants to go out with you again."

Riley didn't know what to say. He was horrified at the thought of ever having to go on another date with Alex!

Back at the dessert cart, the waiter approached Max and Justin. "Do you want me to call your parents?" he asked.

"That would be terrific," Justin answered. "I think they should see this." The brothers' plan had totally worked!

Alex was never going to live this down. Revenge had been officially served.

Chapter Six

Mr. and Mrs. Russo picked up Alex, Justin, and Max from Medium Rare and headed home. As they walked in the front door, Mrs. Russo glared at Alex. "And how long did you think it was going to be before we figured out you didn't know Spanish?"

"I really only needed you to think it until the date was over," Alex explained honestly.

Mr. Russo looked at Alex with disappointment. "You almost exposed magic to the real world," he said with a frown.

"Yes," Alex admitted. "And I've already punished myself because I embarrassed myself in front of Riley, and he probably won't ever text me again." She hoped this argument would work with her dad. She really thought what she had endured already would suffice. There was really nothing her parents could do or say that would make it worse. Or so she thought, anyway.

"And the fact that you two were just *conveniently* down at the restaurant tells me you had something to do with it," Mr. Russo said accusingly, turning his attention to Max and Justin.

Justin tried to explain. "We were on our way to another place," he said nervously. "We stopped there on our way home."

"From where?" Mr. Russo challenged.

"From a place that . . . Max knows the name of," he said quickly, looking over at his little brother.

49

"Pass," Max said. He had a feeling he was in enough trouble. He didn't want to say a word!

"What is going on here?" Mr. Russo demanded.

"Okay, look. Here's what happened—" Justin was about to tell his father everything when Alex interupted him.

"I called them when things started to go wrong," she lied. "They just came down to help. It's not their fault."

Mr. Russo seemed to accept this explanation. "Fine," he said. "For now." He then looked over at Alex, who was still covered in chocolate. "You, go hose off on the balcony."

"Fine," she agreed, and headed outside.

"And you two, clean up when she's done," Mr. Russo told his sons. Their parents left the room, leaving the siblings by themselves.

"Thanks for not ratting us out," Justin said gratefully, when their parents were out of earshot.

"Don't thank me," Alex replied. "I didn't rat you out because I'm going to get even for you guys getting even."

"Oh, no," Max groaned. "Her getting even is way worse than telling." They didn't even want to think about how Alex would try to get revenge. The brothers looked at each other and knew exactly what they had to do.

"Dad, it was us! We gave the elf the chocolate!" they yelled, running up the steps after their father. They would much rather be grounded than see what tricks Alex had up her sleeve!

Alex just stood there laughing. What else could she do? She'd have to come up with some kind of excuse for her crazy behavior the next time she saw Riley. Not that she was all that hopeful. I mean, stuffing your face with chocolate on a first date isn't exactly the smoothest move, she thought.

But at least one good thing came out of it. Alex had definitely learned her lesson. She would make it up to her parents by learning Spanish, even if it meant studying all day— every day!

Alex looked down at her chocolate-stained clothing and sighed. And this time she would learn Spanish *without* the help of a Pocket Elf!

PART
TWO

Chapter One

There were a lot of perks to having a wizard for a father—inheriting his wizard powers was one of them. Having to take wizard lessons, however, was not. But there was no getting out of it. So on this particular Sunday morning, Alex, Justin, and Max Russo gathered grumpily in the lair. It was the secret room in their house where the lessons were held. Usually they had lessons every Tuesday and Thursday after school, but Mr. Russo had added a special Sunday lesson this week in order to get the kids to take their wizard training more seriously.

To try and make it a little more fun, Jerry Russo decided to let the three wizards in training practice new spells. Alex was psyched. She loved trying new things and she had just the spell in mind. Quickly, she tried it . . . and accidentally turned her dad into a goat!

"Okay, Alex, change me back," he demanded, as his kids laughed.

"Oh, but, Daddy, you look so cute as a goat," Alex said sweetly.

"Let's make him eat a tin can!" Max, the youngest Russo sibling, exclaimed. Alex and Justin looked at their dad hopefully.

Mr. Russo still wasn't in a joking mood. "Not funny, Max. Alex, change me back," he bleated.

"Okay, okay," Alex finally said, giving in. "*Huminoza-espinoza*," she chanted. Instantaneously, her father was turned back into a human. Still, the three siblings couldn't stop laughing.

Mr. Russo had had enough. "That's it! You just laughed your way into one hour of study hall. Starting now!" he ordered. The trio took their seats, groaning and muttering. "And that means working on your wizard homework and not messing around. Who's laughing now?" He attempted to laugh, but he still sounded like a goat. Dismayed, Mr. Russo left the room.

"There's something wrong with that spell," Alex noted. "Or maybe it's me." She thought about that for a second. "No, it's got to be the spell," she joked. She *never* made mistakes. She would deal with figuring out the spell later. She had more important things to take care of.

She turned around and opened up her special wizard computer—which looked like an old typewriter, but had a modern computer screen. As it booted up, "WIZ OS 800" appeared on the screen. Wizard computers all had their own operating system.

"What are you doing on the wizard computer?" Max asked his sister.

"Yeah," Justin chimed in, "we're supposed to be doing our homework, not surfing the World Wide Wiz Web."

"I have to do a little shopping," Alex replied. "I like to look good when I'm doing my homework." She looked at the screen, which read, "Witch McCann's No Trip High Heels."

"Oh, this place has the *best* no-trip high heels!" Alex exclaimed. "No matter how high the heels are, it's impossible to twist your ankle. I have to try some on." She hit a key on her computer and the store suddenly appeared right there in the lair!

Her brothers were a bit taken aback when racks of shoes, complete with a saleswoman, suddenly appeared. But Alex wasn't very impressed—with the store *or* the shoes.

"Hmm, they were cuter on-screen," she commented. She clicked a key on the keyboard, and the store suddenly disappeared. She went back to surfing the Internet.

"Oh, look, here's something for Justin!" she exclaimed. This time, she was on a Web site called beyondscales.com, which sold, according to the Web page, "Pet Dragons and More!"

Just then, a salesman and a large table with pets on it appeared. Only these pets had wings!

Alex walked over to the table. "Check it out. Minidragons for sale," she said. But Justin didn't look excited at all. He headed toward the door. "I'm getting out of here because I don't want to get involved. . . ." But suddenly something caught his eye. An adorable beagle gazed up at him. "Oh, that is the cutest little dog I've ever seen!" he exclaimed. He forgot all about leaving and started petting the beagle instead.

"Not *only* is he cute," the salesman said, "but he's also a dragon. That's right, a mythical creature and a dog combined!" he bellowed, waving his hands in the air dramatically. He stopped and gave Alex a serious look. "Now, tell me, how many would you like?"

"We're just looking," Alex replied.

"Well, what will it take for me to get you involved in one of these marvelous little dragon dogs today?" he asked.

Max was so confused. "I don't get it. Is it a dragon or is it a dog?"

"It was charmed to look like a dog so it could exist in the real world," the salesman explained quickly.

"Okay, how are we going to have a dragon dog?" Justin asked. "Mom would totally freak out!"

"He seems friendly," Alex commented,

admiring the creature. "I bet you he's not much of a guard dog." But the dog quickly proved her wrong by barking so loudly he produced a fireball from his mouth! They all gasped.

"That is awesome!" Max exclaimed.

"I like him," Alex said. "He's feisty."

"Eh, dragon in a beagle suit, what's the big deal?" Justin asked. He was over the whole dragon-dog thing already.

"Oh, I'll tell you what the big deal is," the salesman said convincingly. "This dragon dog is on sale for five million cubicks. And because you have a coupon—here, take that," he said, stuffing a coupon into Alex's hand, "it's twenty percent off."

That did it for Alex. "Dude, you should totally get him!" she exclaimed. "He's on sale." Alex never passed up a bargain.

But Justin retreated and suddenly got somber. "I'm sorry. I can't get another dog again. No way. Not after what happened with Willie."

Max looked over at Justin. "Hey, who's Willie?" he asked.

Justin wasn't sure how to tell Max. "He's, uh, he's the dog we had when you were a baby."

"Oh, no. Here come the tears. Or as Justin calls them, his 'allergies,'" Alex teased. Alex wasn't as emotional about Willie as Justin was, but she still felt a little bad at the mention of their old pet.

Justin ignored Alex and pulled out his wallet, out of which unfolded about ten pictures of Willie. He showed them to Max as he spoke. "When I was seven, he, uh, got lost, and I swore I'd never love another dog again." He started to choke up. "I got to go, my . . . allergies are acting up," he finished and ran out the door.

"I'll take him," Alex said, turning to the salesman. "Justin's going to love me for this."

"But Justin just said that he doesn't want a dog," Max protested.

Alex disregarded this information. "Trust me. Justin wants a dog."

The salesman, of course, concurred. "Trust her. Justin wants a dog."

"Here's five million cubicks in U.S. currency," Alex said, handing him the cash. She always saved her allowance. The salesman looked impressed that she handed him exactly the right amount of money.

Alex caught his glance and smiled knowingly. "Oh, I know the exchange rate. I order from the Abercrombie and Witch catalog all the time."

The salesman smiled mischievously. "Your five-second warranty just ended," the salesman said, right before he and his store disappeared into thin air! All that was left was the Russos' new pet.

"Well," Alex said, kneeling down next to the

dog, "let's go find a cute doggie sweater to match that cute doggie face." Alex patted the dog's head and headed back to the computer to do some more online shopping.

"Come on," Max called. "Come on, doggie."

But the dog did not want to play with Max. He headed right over to Alex's notebook and barked another ball of fire, scorching her homework. Alex looked on, slightly shocked. "My dog burnt my homework," she quipped, as she reached for the fire extinguisher. "That'll be a new one."

Chapter Two

Later that day, Alex took their new dog for a walk. She returned home and was about to open the front door to the apartment all the way. She stopped, her hand on the knob. Peeking in, she looked for her parents and Justin. She knew he was going to be so excited to see their new pet, and wanted to surprise him, but she couldn't have her parents see her first. Spotting him in the living room, she opened the door further. "Justin, you're going to love this," she called out. "Close your eyes."

Justin looked at Alex curiously. "Okay," he said uncertainly, "but I'm not going to taste anything."

Alex ushered the dog into the living room. "Ta-da!" she announced.

Justin's eyes widened as he found himself staring at the little creature they had just argued about earlier that day. "Alex, what's that dragon dog doing here? I told you, I don't want another pet."

"Well, I think you do, and so did the dragon seller," Alex replied calmly.

"Of course he did, he's a dragon seller," Justin retorted. "And besides, what are we going to tell Mom and Dad?"

"Mom and Dad don't have to know he's a dragon," Alex explained. "I'll just say that I found a dog. Because it's a dog, and it looks like a dog . . ." She paused and added as an aside, ". . . that barks fire."

66

"Okay, I appreciate what you're trying to do for me here, but I can't go down this path again," Justin said, beginning to get upset. "And . . . and besides, you know about my allergies."

"It's crying," Alex said flatly. She wasn't going to pretend that Justin had allergies any longer.

"I'm allergic to sadness!" Justin argued.

Seeing how emotional her brother was, Alex decided to finally tell Justin the truth. "Look, I know losing Willie broke your heart. But the truth is, he didn't run away and get lost. He . . . he got out," she said slowly, "because . . . because I kind of *let* him out."

"It was you?" Justin couldn't believe his ears! "Mom and Dad told me it was the pizza-delivery guy. I haven't eaten pizza in, like, eight years!"

Alex let out a big sigh. She'd been keeping

this secret for a really long time, and it felt good to finally tell Justin the truth. "Don't be mad. I was five. I wanted to take Willie for a walk, and he wanted to go for a run," she explained. She sounded, Justin thought, *apologetic*. Which was really not like Alex at all.

"You're saying you feel guilty?" Justin suggested, raising an eyebrow. Alex almost never admitted when she had done anything wrong.

"Rarely," she admitted. "But, yes."

"All right," he said, accepting Alex's version of an apology. Then he turned to the dog—his dog—with a whole new attitude. "Hey, buddy," he said, petting him. "That's a good boy." He smiled at his new pet. "Oh, he just did that thing with his nose like Willie did," Justin exclaimed. "Do you like your new home, boy?" he asked, using his own hands to make the dog nod his head like a human. "He can nod!" Justin looked at his sister. "Thanks, Alex. He's awesome," he said happily.

Just then Mr. and Mrs. Russo came up the stairs from their restaurant, The Waverly Sub Station, which was located just downstairs. That made it super convenient—which wasn't always a great thing. It meant it made it way too easy for the kids to help out by working shifts at the restaurant.

"Ah! I love a good lunch rush," Theresa Russo said as she took off her apron and walked into the kitchen.

"Me, too," Mr. Russo said. "I just wish everyone wouldn't show up at once," he said with a sigh. He stopped, noticing the dog. "What's that?" he asked Justin curiously.

"A dog. Just a dog," he said nervously. He didn't want to reveal that the dog was in fact a dragon as well!

"Yeah," Mrs. Russo said slowly. "What's it doing here?" she asked.

Alex quickly stepped in. "I found it wandering alone on Waverly Place. Lonely.

Looking for a home," she said with a smile.

"It's destiny," Justin urged. "We have to keep it."

Mr. Russo kneeled down and started to pet the dog. "Hey, buddy. How you doing, boy? Good boy. Speak!"

Suddenly, Max ran in and yelled, "No! Don't speak! Don't speak! Shh!" He was worried the dog would breathe another fireball.

"Why not?" Mr. Russo asked.

"Because if he speaks, there'll be fire," Max said, not realizing that Alex and Justin hadn't let their parents in on this little—but rather important—piece of information. Justin tried to cut him off, but it was too late.

"What?" Mr. Russo asked in confusion.

"What Max is trying to say is that he's saving his voice for those barking-dog albums," Alex blurted out. She had had to come up with something, but even she had to admit it was a really lame explanation.

"He does a mean Bon Jovi," Justin added.

Mr. Russo looked at the dog and grinned. He was already leaning toward keeping him. All he had to do now was convince his wife. "Well, see, he's multitalented. I . . . I think we should keep him, Theresa," he offered.

"Oh, we can't keep a lost dog," she replied. "Someone's probably looking for him."

"Oh, that is *so* true," Alex agreed earnestly. "You're right, Mom. And we should probably put flyers up in the city, so we can find its rightful owner."

"Really? But he's so cute!" Mr. Russo exclaimed. "Come on, Alex, you pick now to be responsible?" he pressed his daughter. This was so unlike her. What he didn't know was that she had a plan, as usual.

"Absolutely. We'll . . . we'll scour the city for the owner, and on the off chance that we come up short, only then will we keep the dog," she said with conviction, knowing full well that no such person would show up.

"Hmm," her mother said curiously. "That's, uh, very mature, Alex. I'm proud of you."

Justin pulled Alex aside. He didn't understand what she was up to either. "Oh, so that's been your plan all along, huh? Play with my fragile heart and then crush it. What happens if the rightful dog owner comes along and sees the LOST DOG sign?" he asked.

"No one's going to claim it because it's not lost *or* a dog. And you're the smart one?" she asked sarcastically.

"You're right," Justin admitted. "I'm sorry. I just got a little panicked over what happened with Willie."

"Let it go," Alex said defensively. "I was five!"

Mr. Russo, meanwhile, was very excited about their furry houseguest. "As long as he's here, what should we call him? Ooh, I know! Here's an idea: Spot. No, wait, Paws. Ooh, Patches!" he exclaimed.

Mrs. Russo suddenly piped up. "I think you should call it Dragon."

The kids looked at each other, panicked. Did their mom know that the dog was really a dragon? This was *so* not good.

"What? Why would we do that?" Justin asked quickly.

"Yeah. Why?" Alex asked, laughing nervously.

"Because it's a dragon," their mother replied simply.

Justin and Alex exchanged uneasy glances. They looked at Max. He must have been the one who told her.

"I swear, I didn't say anything," their little brother protested.

"Its name is right here on its tag," Mrs. Russo said, showing them the tag. "Its name is 'Dragon.'"

The three siblings looked at one another and sighed. That had been way too close!

"The name Dragon is on its tag," Justin said loudly, with great relief.

"Oh," Alex said at the very same time, also too loudly. "I love the name Dragon. Good eye, Mom!" she exclaimed. "It's like it was meant to be. Okay, let's talk about something else now," she said, trying desperately to change the subject. Their new pet was already proving to be a lot more than Alex bargained for!

Chapter Three

Alex headed down to the Waverly Sub Station to start posting flyers. She had to make it look as if she were trying to find the dog's rightful owner. If they didn't make it look genuine, her parents were sure to get suspicious. She had finished putting up the flyers and decided to go outside to ask the guys who ran the newspaper stand if she could post one there, too. The more flyers she posted, the better she would look to her parents!

"Hey, Charlie," she said to a person holding a giant open newspaper in front of his covered face. "Can I hang one of these 'found dog' signs on your stand?"

But it wasn't Charlie. "What's in it for me, sweetheart?" responded what turned out to be a little kid named Frankie. He put down the paper.

Alex was confused. "Where's Charlie?" she asked.

"Let's just say Charlie went to the bank to get the candy he owes me. And by 'candy' I mean 'money,'" he said, trying to act tough.

"Yeah, I kind of figured that when you said 'bank,'" she retorted. "Um, can I hang one of these signs on your stand?" she asked again. "I'll give you a Bronxstrami-Swiss on rye," she offered in exchange.

"How about a Bronxstrami-Swiss and a kiss?" Frankie asked, leaning closer to Alex.

Alex rolled her eyes. "How about a Bronxstrami-Swiss and a bowl of soup?" she bargained, dismissing any chance of a kiss.

"Cup of soup, foot-long, no cheaping out on the cheese, and a meaningful hug," he negotiated.

"No hug," Alex said sternly. "Done."

"You'll come around," Frankie said, as Alex taped the sign to the newsstand. "They always do."

"Well, I don't know who *they* are, but I'm not one of them," Alex huffed. She went back into the restaurant.

Just then, Max and Justin walked up to the newsstand with Dragon. "He's just like Willie," Justin was telling Max. "He likes dog treats, squeak toys, and toilet water." He smiled at his new pet. "Let me get a picture of you, boy. Sit," he commanded. The dog responded to Justin's command and sat down. "This will go great in the activities chapter of the photo album I'm putting together," Justin told Max.

"Cute pup," Frankie noted. "What's his name?"

Max turned toward him. He had met Frankie the day before, when he went down to buy a newspaper for Mrs. Russo. "Dragon," Max told him and then felt the need to explain. "Not . . . not because he is a dragon. No, because there's no such thing as dragons," he said nervously. "I should stop talking," he said, reprimanding himself.

"Does he fetch?" Frankie asked.

"No," Justin said. "He doesn't fetch." Frankie grabbed a ball and poised his arm in the air, ready to throw it. "You probably don't want to do that," Justin said anxiously. But it was too late.

"Go get it, Dragon!" Frankie yelled as he threw the ball, not heeding Justin's advice. Dragon's wings popped out, and he was off. Seconds later, he returned with the ball. "Were those wings?" Frankie asked in disbelief.

"Yeah, good one, Frankie." Max scoffed. "A dog with wings."

"Yeah," Justin chimed in. "Dragon's just like Michael Jordan. Every once in a while a superstar comes along and elevates the whole game," he said with a dismissive laugh.

Frankie studied the ball that Dragon had returned to him. "Why is it burnt?" he asked them.

"It's . . . it's not burnt," Justin stuttered. "It's just . . . it's just like toast. You just . . . brush off all the black stuff, and it's good as new. See?"

Frankie wasn't completely convinced that Justin was telling the truth. "All right," Frankie said suspiciously. "It works for now. But something doesn't smell right on Waverly Place," he added.

Taking the moment to get out of there, Justin and Max headed home. When they were safely away from Frankie's prying eyes, they took Dragon out on the balcony. They knew they'd have to train him to act more like a regular dog, and fast. Sure, he could sit on command, but Dragon would have to do a lot better than that!

"That was a close call," Justin said to Max. "We got to train Dragon to act like a normal dog." He suddenly had an idea. "Oh, there's a cat," he said to Dragon. Although there was no cat in sight, he wanted to see if Dragon would listen to his commands. "Go get him!" The dog took off in the direction Justin was pointing to.

"Oh, wow! He did it! But it was kind of cooler when he would just—" Max started to say "fly," but Justin interrupted him.

"Shh! Don't say F-L-Y around him," he urged, spelling out the word.

"F-L-Y," Max said, trying to figure out what his brother had spelled. "Oh, fly!" he exclaimed. Immediately, Dragon's wings popped out. Soon he was soaring above them.

"Oh, fly," Justin said sarcastically.

Just then, Mrs. Russo stepped out onto the terrace to water her plants. "Boy, it's so hot out here," Mrs. Russo commented, not noticing the dog orbiting directly above her.

"Fly! Fly!" Justin said again, hoping the dog would stay up in the air.

"What?" Mrs. Russo asked.

"Oh, nothing. Uh, I said there's a lot of flies out here," Justin said nervously.

"Where?" she asked, looking up.

"Not up there," Justin said, trying to distract her. "I meant ants."

Mrs. Russo looked down. "Oh, I hate ants," she said, wrinkling her nose in disgust. Luckily, his mother hadn't caught on.

Justin knew he had to get his mom out of there before she spotted Dragon. He directed his mom back inside, encouraging her to go get the ant spray.

As his mom disappeared into the house,

Justin breathed a sigh of relief. That was a close one, he thought to himself. First, Dragon brought a burnt ball back to Frankie and then he started flying right above his mom's head. Whew, Justin thought. Having a dog that can fly is a lot of work!

Chapter Four

"Come on, guys," Justin said impatiently to Alex and Max as they walked home from school the next day. "We've got to go check on Dragon." They planned on stopping at the Waverly Sub Station to say hello to their parents, but then they were hightailing it upstairs. They were anxious to see how their new pet was doing. "Yeah, we've never left him alone before," Alex said worriedly. She was walking superfast, hoping to find Dragon doing regular dog things, like playing with a squeak toy or gnawing on a bone. Not dragon-dog things, like flying!

"I'm sure he's just fine," Max said calmly. "And if anyone messed with him, he'd just breathe fire," Max said with a grin.

Alex and Justin looked at each other. That was exactly what they were hoping Dragon *wasn't* doing. "Yeah, that's what we're worried about," Alex said nervously.

The three siblings finally arrived at the restaurant. Justin rushed through the dining area, hurrying past his parents and heading up the stairs. "Hey, guys," he said quickly. "Got to go check on Dragon!"

"Wait! Justin!" Mrs. Russo called after him.

"Justin!" Mr. Russo shouted, but Justin had already gone upstairs and was out of earshot. "I'll go tell him," he said to his wife. He looked down sadly.

"What's the matter?" Alex asked.

"Um, those flyers you put up worked," her dad explained. "Dragon's rightful owner came by and picked him up while you kids were at school."

"What rightful owner?" Alex questioned. How could this have happened? *They* were Dragon's owners! She had paid for him fair and square.

Just then, Justin returned downstairs. "Hey, guys. Where's Dragon?" He had looked everywhere for the dog and couldn't find him.

Mrs. Russo hesitated before telling her son the news. She knew how hard it had been on him when she had to tell him about Willie. "H . . . his owner claimed him," she stuttered.

"His owner?" he asked skeptically. He looked at Alex, clearly confused.

Mrs. Russo sighed. She didn't know what to say. "Honey, I am so sorry. I know how much you loved him."

"He's gone?" Justin asked sadly. His voice shook a little as the news sank in. "There's so much we didn't get to do."

But it was Alex who felt the worst of all. After all, *she* was the one who had convinced Justin to get the dog. And it was also her idea to put up fake flyers. This was all her fault. "Justin, I'm sorry," she said honestly.

"Thanks a lot," he replied sadly. "This is why I didn't want to get close to another dog. You did it to me again." He went back upstairs.

Alex sighed. Her brother was right. She had done it to him—again. She needed fresh air and time to think. Heading downstairs, she wandered outside, not sure what to do next. Then she realized that she probably should do something about all the flyers she had put up the day before. She walked around and started crossing out the word "Found" on her "Found Dog" signs and replacing it with the word "Lost." All of a sudden, she spotted Frankie.

"You lost your found dog?" he asked. "Why don't you rest your head on Frankie's shoulder and tell him all about it," he suggested.

"I would, but I don't have time for you to get a ladder," she joked. Then she changed her tone. "This is serious. Someone claimed Dragon. But whoever it was, it wasn't the real owner."

"That's weird, because he looked like a dog lover," Frankie said.

Alex looked over at him. "You saw him? Who was he?" she questioned.

Frankie saw another opportunity to negotiate. "You got a meatball sub with my name on it?" he asked.

"I'll give you the bread now, and you'll get your meatballs after we find the dognapper," she replied quickly. No one could out-negotiate Alex.

Frankie agreed. He never could resist a sandwich from the Waverly Sub Station. "The guy came out with your dog and brought this," he said, pointing to a stack of pamphlets. It was a brochure about an upcoming dog show.

"The Hudson Dog Show? When is it?" Alex asked.

"Why don't you buy a copy and find out?" Frankie suggested.

"I have to *buy* it?" she asked.

"Do I come into your restaurant, lick a sandwich, and leave? That'll be eight dollars, please." He smiled confidently.

"Okay," Alex said, grabbing a pamphlet. She handed Frankie some money, but quickly spotted the date and location of the event on the brochure and took the money back. "It's today! I'd like to return this for a refund," she gloated.

But her gloating quickly subsided. She

needed a plan—and quickly! She had to admit, even though she had gotten the dog for Justin, she was pretty attached to him already, too. And maybe, just maybe, she could redeem herself with Justin after all.

Chapter Five

A short while later, Justin and Max had come back downstairs to work their after-school shift at the restaurant. Justin, however, couldn't focus on anything but the sad news about Dragon. He was so busy staring at a photo of his dog that he didn't even notice the customer standing at the counter. Finally, the man cleared his throat.

Justin was startled out of his reverie. "May I help you?" he asked.

"Can I get a *hound* of corned beef?" the man asked. Or, at least, that was what Justin *thought* he had heard.

"I'm sorry, did you say 'hound?'" Justin asked.

"No," the man replied, looking confused.

"Oh," Justin said sadly. He could've sworn the customer had said the word "hound" instead of "pound." He turned to Max with a frown. "Man, everything reminds me of Dragon. Everything!"

"That's rough," Max said.

"*Ruff*," Justin said quietly. "That's what *he* used to say." He was looking off into space when he realized that the customer was still waiting for his order. Embarrassed, he quickly cleared his throat. "Um, a pound of corned beef, coming up!"

Mr. Russo, who was waiting on tables, approached the counter. "Max, can you go in the back and grab some more to-go pups?"

Justin couldn't believe this. "*Pups?*" he asked his father incredulously.

"No. To-go *cups*," Mr. Russo clarified.

"Oh," Justin said. He felt like he was going crazy!

When Mr. Russo looked to his younger son for some kind of explanation of Justin's strange behavior, Max sighed. "All he can think about is Dragon," he said.

Justin let out a big sigh, too. He didn't know what he was going to do. Even though he'd only had Dragon as a pet for one day, he missed him so much.

At that moment, Alex ran through the door. She looked at her brothers excitedly. "Justin, Max. You're coming with me," she commanded. "We're getting Dragon back."

Justin couldn't believe the good news! He took off his apron and headed for the other side of the counter. "Dad, we're taking a break," he called out.

"Come on, you guys! Hurry!" Alex pleaded, already running back outside.

"*Furry*?" Justin asked, racing to catch up to his sister. "He was so furry!"

The two brothers ran out the door and followed Alex. They had no idea where she was taking them, but one thing was clear—they weren't coming back without Dragon!

The three siblings finally reached their destination—the Hudson Dog Show! Alex was sure Dragon was somewhere inside. She let out a sigh of relief as they approached the entrance. "Three tickets for the dog show, please," she said to a man at the check-in table. A female security guard standing next to the table answered her instead.

"It's sold out," the woman reported.

"What?" Alex asked in disbelief. This was *not* a scenario that she had imagined.

"Apparently a lot of people like watching dogs run around on plastic grass," the guard replied in a bored tone. "No dog, no way in." Then, into her walkie-talkie she uttered, "Large fries. See if there's a toy included. Over." She was much more interested in her food order than she was in letting them into the show. And after all, they didn't have a dog with them. Rules were rules.

Justin wasn't at all concerned, though. His sister had a knack for getting out of situations like these. "Alex will talk us in," he said to Max confidently. "She's a master."

"I totally understand," Alex said to the guard. She turned to her brothers. "Come on, guys. It's not happening."

"What?" Justin cried. He couldn't believe this! She had just given up? Just like that? That wasn't at all like Alex!

"That's it?" he asked, his voice filled with exasperation. "We're not getting my dog back?"

"Of *course* we're getting your dog back,"

Alex replied. "We just need to get a dog first," she said slowly.

Max eyed his sister. He knew that tone of voice. "Where are we going to find a dog without an owner?" he asked.

Alex didn't answer. Instead, she put her plan into action. Remembering the spell she had used to turn her father into a goat during their last wizard lesson, she used the same spell on Max. And within seconds, Max was transformed into a dog. They were able to stroll right into the dog show.

"It worked," Alex said proudly, standing with Justin and Max, who was now on all fours and had taken the form of a small dachshund. "We're in."

"Let's get Max back," Justin said.

"Okay," Alex replied reluctantly. "*Huminoza-espinoza*," she said, repeating the spell.

Suddenly, Max reappeared. He quickly stood up. But while he looked normal, he was acting strangely. "Being a dog is weird," he said. "All you want to do is just chase your tail," he added, scratching his head the way a dog would.

Alex was a little worried. "I don't think I got the spell quite right," she admitted.

"What makes you say that?" Max asked, sniffing the ground. He spotted a chew toy and walked over to it. Then, to Justin's and Alex's surprise, he picked up the toy with his teeth and shook it around in his mouth!

Oh, boy, Alex thought to herself. Maybe I shouldn't have tried that spell after all! She was distracted by the problem at hand by a familiar sight.

"Look!" she said excitedly. "There he is!" She had just spotted Dragon. She was so relieved. After all, she had come here on a tip from Frankie. The truth was, she didn't really know if Dragon would be here, but it was the only lead she had.

"Dragon?" Justin asked tearfully.

"*And* the dragon seller," Alex noted, suddenly spotting him as well. "He stole Dragon back," she realized. Alex was so angry. She couldn't believe the nerve of the salesman! Suddenly, she knew exactly what was going on!

"Come on," she said to her brothers. She was determined to put an end to this here and now. "Let's go get Dragon."

Alex stormed over to the salesman and confronted him. "Hey, you're a thief!" she shouted accusingly. "You sold us that dog and then stole it back!"

"It's the circle of life, children," the salesman explained matter-of-factly.

"We want our dog back," Alex demanded.

"Look, kid," he said, "you played the game, and you lost. You know what? You go home, and the money you spent on the dog was a lesson well learned. You're welcome." He was smiling condescendingly, and the trio didn't appreciate that very much.

"No deal," Justin said, shaking his head. "We're taking Dragon home."

"I don't think so," the salesman said with a smirk. He snapped his fingers, and the dog disappeared into thin air. "Look, he's gone."

But Max knew this wasn't the case. Even though he was back in human form, he still had some doglike qualities left. "Oh, he's not gone," he said, sniffing the air. "He's still here. I can smell him." He looked around. There were dogs everywhere! It wasn't going to be easy.

Alex thought of an idea. If Max had a canine ability for scent, he'd be able to sniff out Dragon among all the other dogs!

"All we have to do is get Max to smell the beagles," Alex said to Justin.

"How do you know he's still a beagle?" the salesman taunted. "I changed him from a dragon into a beagle. I can change him into any dog that I want. I can change him into a terrier mix, into an Irish bloodhound, or into whatever that is," he said, pointing to a tiny dog with frizzy hair. "Oh, it's not that," he said with a laugh. "That is a rat with a blow-dry."

Alex leaned into her little brother. "Max, can you sniff out Dragon?"

"I can try," Max said earnestly. He started sniffing around the entire room, approaching each dog and dismissing them quickly. "Nope, not this one. Oh, definitely not this one," he commented, sniffing right near the same security guard they had met earlier at the entrance. She was not impressed with Max's strange behavior.

"Are you through?" the security guard asked. "Freak," she said. Then she pushed a button on her walkie-talkie and said, "Bob, bring around the security trailer. I got a sniffer."

A few moments later, Max found himself being hauled out of the room by a guard. All he could do was continue to sniff with his nose in the air, still trying to locate Dragon. As Alex watched helplessly, she felt anger bubble up. She couldn't believe her plan hadn't worked!

"Great," Alex said. "How are we going to find Dragon now? Our sniffer just got thrown in dog-show jail."

Chapter Six

Justin and Alex stood quietly for a moment, trying to come up with a new plan. Suddenly, Justin smiled.

"Oh, I know!" he exclaimed. "Dragons don't chase cats."

Alex immediately caught on to Justin's train of thought. "If we had a cat, all the dogs would go wild chasing it, except for Dragon." This was a good plan. No, it was a great plan.

"I'm on it. I'll change myself into a cat," she said excitedly.

"But you always mess up the spell," Justin told her.

"Do you have a better idea?" Alex scoffed. She didn't even bother to wait a second for his answer. "Didn't think so," she gloated. "*Animoza-espinoza*."

Suddenly, Alex was gone and an adorable cat stood in her place . . . but only for a moment. The cat then morphed into a giant tiger!

"How do I look?" she asked Justin, prancing around. "Cute, huh?" She had no idea that she wasn't still a regular cat.

But it didn't take long for the crowd to notice there was a giant tiger loose among the pampered pooches. Chaos broke out immediately.

"Oh! A tiger!" someone screamed, running out of the room.

"Is that a tiger?" another woman shrieked.

"Uh, I think you messed up the spell again," Justin commented to Alex.

"Oh, no!" Alex lamented. "I've got to get that spell right."

Just then, the security guard approached them, still holding on to Max. She spoke into her walkie-talkie. "Bob, bring the catnip. All of it," she said, before remembering something else she wanted to tell Bob. "Make sure I get extra ketchup," she added. Apparently, even the presence of a tiger at a dog show wasn't enough to take her mind off dinner. The man they assumed was Bob walked into the room a moment later. He handed a bag of food to the guard. But as soon as he spotted the tiger, he ran away.

"Bob?" the female guard yelled after him. He'd forgotten the extra ketchup! She headed out of the room to look for him.

Suddenly, they spotted a beagle wearing a

familiar-looking name tag. It was Dragon! He ran toward Justin and jumped into his arms. "Dragon!" Justin shouted happily. "Oh, good boy!"

But their reunion was short-lived. The cunning salesman walked toward them holding a dog cage in his hand. He put the cage down on the floor directly next to another cage and opened the door for Dragon. "You found him. Good work," he told the trio.

"Come on," he called to Dragon. The dog obeyed and ran right into the cage.

Alex, who was still in the form of a tiger, let out the biggest roar she could muster, in the hope of scaring the salesman so he would give Dragon back to them. Justin and Max played along, pretending to be frightened. "Scary!" Justin shrieked, as Max covered his mouth in feigned fright.

"I still know it's you, kid," the salesman said to Tiger Alex.

"Eh, it's worth a shot. *Huminoza-espinoza*," she chanted. Alex immediately reappeared, but started to lick her own arms the way a cat would lick its paws. That spell was giving her a headache—not to mention a furball!

Justin was fed up. None of their planning or scheming had gotten them anywhere. He just wanted his dog back.

"You know, I'd like to stay and chat, but I've got a dog here I have to sell," the salesman said quickly.

But Alex had one more trick up her sleeve. "Not so fast," she said to him. "Look, you were right before. We've learned our lesson. No hard feelings."

"I have hard feelings," Justin complained.

But Alex ignored him. She had another ploy that she hoped would work.

"We're just kids, and we should probably thank someone like you for giving us street smarts and making us more cautious with future purchases," she told the salesman.

"Yeah," he said, clearly enjoying the compliment. "I am a pretty good teacher," the dishonest salesman admitted.

"So, thank you and have a good day. But, oh," Alex said, picking up the cage that was beside her feet and handing it to him, "don't forget your cage." She gave him a winning smile.

Distracted by Alex's new approach, the salesman accepted the cage that she handed him. "You know, I never thought I would say this to a customer, but it has been a pleasure scamming you," he said in a menacing tone. Suddenly, there was a big poof of smoke, and he and Dragon were gone!

"What are you doing? You let him get away with Dragon!" Justin shouted, his face turning red.

"You're right, I'm sorry," Alex apologized calmly. She bent down to unlatch the door on the other dog cage that was still on the floor. "Now all you have is . . . Dragon!" The dog excitedly ran out of the cage.

"Dragon!" Justin exclaimed happily.

Max was confused. "Alex, how'd you do that?"

"I just made him take the wrong cage, like I do with you guys and our lunches," she said, smiling.

Both boys nodded. Alex had a habit of switching lunches when she didn't like the kind of sandwich she had. They had fallen victim more than once.

"But who'd he take?" Max asked.

"The blow-dried rat," Alex said proudly. "I saw the cage right there, I thought on my feet, and I out-conned the con wizard. I'm good."

Back in their living room, the family sat around admiring their pet. The siblings had just finished telling their parents all about the dog show as well as the truth about their new pet.

"So, can we keep him?" Justin asked his parents hopefully, when they were finished. He held his breath, waiting.

"Oh, I don't know, honey," his mother said skeptically.

"Max will feed him every day," Alex eagerly volunteered. "And Justin will give him a bath and walk him."

"What will you do?" Justin asked Alex.

"I'm doing it. I'm coordinating what you guys do," Alex said proudly.

"Actually," Mr. Russo said to his wife, "pets *do* teach responsibility."

"Well, I don't see what harm he could do," Mrs. Russo said, finally giving in.

Justin was so excited to hear the news! "Come on, Dragon. Let's go up to my room."

Dragon quickly followed up the stairs behind him.

Alex smiled to herself. Once again, she had

pulled off an elaborate plan with great success. *And* she had even made Justin happy in the meantime. Now that was the work of a true wizard in training!

Something magical is on the way!
Look for the next book in the
Wizards of Waverly Place series.

In Your Face

Adapted by Heather Alexander

Based on the series created by Todd J. Greenwald

Part One is based on the episode, "Pop Me and We Both Go Down," Written by Vince Cheung & Ben Montanio

Part Two is based on the episode, "First Kiss," Written by Vince Cheung & Ben Montanio

Alex Russo pulled her berry-flavored lip gloss out of her new leather handbag. She swiped it over her lips and then reached for her mini-mirror. She glanced at herself. Perfect! She stretched her arms up over her head and skipped into the Waverly Sub Station, her family's restaurant. Her younger brother, Max, stumbled in behind her, a heavy backpack slung over each shoulder.

"Hey, how was school?" their mom called from behind the counter. Theresa Russo gave a little laugh when she spotted her youngest son. "Max! Why are you carrying Alex's backpack like that?"

With the back of his hand, twelve-year-old Max wiped the sweat off his forehead. "She told me my backpack was bending my spine, so she gave me hers to even it out."

"Let's check," Alex said brightly. She slipped her backpack off his right shoulder. She eyed Max critically. "There. All straight. You're welcome."

"Alex," her father scolded. "Your brother is not your pack mule."

"Yeah, I'm not your pack mule!" Max echoed. It was easier standing up to Alex with his parents around.

"I'm sorry, Maxy," Alex apologized. She

handed her backpack to him again. "Could you take this upstairs for me?"

"Sure," Max answered automatically. He headed upstairs to their family's apartment. Halfway up the stairs, he cringed. Alex had done it to him again! Why couldn't he say no to his devious sister?

Sixteen-year-old Justin Russo hurried through the front doors of the restaurant. "Best day at school ever!" he cried.

Mrs. Russo looked up from the submarine sandwich she was making. "Oh, they found the guy that was putting peanut butter in your locker?"

"No, but this made me forget about that," Justin replied. "Okay, so I'm in biology, right? Mr. Medina has us pick lab partners, and, like always, my partner ends up being the frog I'm dissecting." Justin hung his head in embarrassment. He didn't run with the popular crowd at school—to put it nicely.

Alex waved her hand. "I have the opposite problem. Everybody wants me to be their lab partner."

Justin chuckled at his sister. "But you don't take biology."

"That's what I keep telling those guys!" Alex beamed. Popularity was her middle name.

"Anyway," Justin said, continuing his story, "in walks this brand-new girl, and she is the hottest thing I've ever seen in my life."

Jerry Russos' eyes opened wide and he leaned over the counter. "Eva Longoria goes to your school?"

"Eva Longoria?" Mrs. Russo asked her husband suspiciously.

Mr. Russo gave an embarrassed laugh. "Kids love Eva Longoria. It's . . . ah . . ." He blushed, realizing he'd just stuck his foot in his mouth. "Continue, son," he said, hoping to change the subject.

"So Mr. Medina assigns the beautiful Miranda Hampson to be my lab partner—"

"Miranda Hampson?" Alex interrupted. "Isn't she that new Goth girl in the eleventh grade?"

Justin shook his head. "She's not Goth," he insisted. "She just likes wearing black and dark makeup, and listens to bands that are kind of scary."

Alex smiled. Her geeky older brother was *so* not clued in. "Oh. So not Goth. But Goth," she teased. She perched herself on one of the spinning stools in front of the counter.

"You're missing my point." Justin gritted his teeth. Alex could be such a know-it-all sometimes. "I'm in the tenth grade. She's an older woman."

"Attaboy!" Mr. Russo walked over and slapped Justin on the back. "Like your mother."

Mrs. Russo glared at her husband.

"Hold on, now," Justin said, sliding between his parents. "The story gets even better. So, me and my Miran—that's my cute nickname for her—actually, yeah, Miran—" Justin cleared his throat dramatically. "—accidentally reached for the scalpel at the same time and our hands touched, and she didn't pull away for three seconds." He smiled. "How's that for a great day?"

Alex twirled on her stool. She pointed toward a girl dressed all in black walking through the front door. "Oh, look. Miranda's here. I guess your great day's still going on—or coming to a tragic end." She delighted in the look of shock on Justin's face. "Let's watch, boys and girls."

Justin nervously cleared his throat. It was one thing to talk to Miranda in biology class over the comfort of dissecting a frog. It was another to have her here—now—standing in his family's restaurant with Alex and his parents as an audience. "Hey, Miran." He tried to sound upbeat but not too excited.

Miranda wrinkled her forehead. "Who's Miran?"

"You. Remember?" Justin laughed. Please let her remember, he prayed.

"Oh." She tucked a piece of dark hair dyed with long, white streaks behind her triple-pierced ear.

"I called you that in lab?" Justin reminded her.

Miranda nodded. "Oh, right. I thought you were swallowing and talking at the same time."

"He does generate a lot of saliva," Alex piped up from behind her.

"I have overactive glands," Justin explained. "We're looking into it."

"It was worse when he was a baby," Mr. Russo added with a chuckle. "We had to wrap his head in a diaper."

"Excuse me one second," Justin said to Miranda. He shot his dad a warning glance.

Mr. Russo caught Justin's eye and got to work pretending to be busy refilling ketchup bottles.

Justin turned back to Miranda. "Do you need to copy my biology notes or something?" Justin was used to kids asking for help with homework.

"Oh, no. No, I—I just came to ask you something," she smiled. "Are you going to the junior prom?"

"Nah," he replied. "I already told them I don't want to work lights this year." He didn't get why the smart kids at school *always* had to be the tech guys.

Miranda giggled. "You are so funny."

Justin laughed nervously. He hadn't tried to be funny.

"No, I mean, would you like to go to the prom with me?" Miranda asked. She took a deep breath. "I'm—I'm new at school, and I don't know a lot of guys, and you seem very nice," she stammered.

"Me?" Justin was momentarily frozen. A girl had just asked him out? To the prom? And not just any girl, but Miranda! He never thought he stood a chance with a girl like Miranda—not without magic skills. He smiled to himself. Miranda was actually far-out enough to, maybe, not be freaked out that he came from a family of wizards who could do magic spells. Of course, he knew he couldn't tell her about that. It was a BIG secret. He'd have to continue pretending he was just a normal guy. Suddenly, he jolted awake from his daydream. *Normal guys answered girls who asked them out!* he realized. "Well, uh, you know. I'll have to check my schedule and—"

"Are you trying to be cool?" Miranda interrupted.

Justin shrugged. "Yeah."

"Don't do that," she said. "I'm really tired of cool guys," she explained.

Justin laughed. "Don't worry, because I'm *so* not cool."

He could hear Alex snicker behind him, but he didn't care. He was going to the junior prom with Miranda Hampson! Nothing could beat that.

Get More of Your Favorite Pop Star!

Bonus:
8 postcards to
send to friends!

Includes 8 full-color postcards!

**Includes 12 posters
of the show's stars!**

**Collect all the stories
about Hannah Montana!**

DISNEY PRESS
AN IMPRINT OF DISNEY BOOK GROUP

www.disneybooks.com

Available wherever
books are sold

Keep Rockin'!

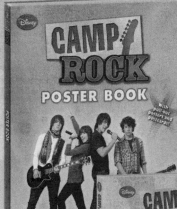

Includes color photos of the stars!

www.disneybooks.com

Available wherever books are sold

Disney PRESS
AN IMPRINT OF DISNEY BOOK GROUP